Letter from the author:

This series was inspired by and is meant to honor my son, Will. His adventurous spirit and pure heart are unmatched. I learn from him daily. My hope is that you too shall get lost in his adventures and live briefly in his pure world.

Please note, the dog, Max, that actively participates in his adventures, was Will's service dog of 9 years. We miss him beyond words and will be forever grateful he was part of our "Will's World.

I'd like to thank the friends and family that helped me with this story. I don't know if I would have had the guts to finish without you.

Thank you for coming along on our adventure.
I am deeply humbled.
Meredith

"Two shorten the road"- If someone is truly by our side, our journey becomes easier. Irish saying. Author unknown.

Celtic Background and pronunciations:

Aine – ('awnya) – Faery queen – Known as "Aine of the Light"

Feasts were held in her honor as late as 1879. This was to ensure good crops.

Niall – (Niall) – male name, meaning "cloud"

Lorcan – male name, meaning "fierce"

Traditional Celtic foods are curds, milk, cheese, and rabbit stew

Hi! I'm Will and this is my dog, Max.
Today we are going on an adventure!

My whole life I've had dreams of making friends with magical faeries and flying on huge, colorful dragons.

Last night, my dream was different. I learned something new. This time I saw the path to The Welcoming Tree. To get to the Land of Faeries and Dragons you must pass through the tree. There is a secret code needed to do this, and I learned that too.

We are walking on the wooded path, in the forest, and should be there soon.

Look! There's the Welcoming Tree!

The entrance to the Land of Faeries and Dragons!

Let's Do This Thing! Come on Max!

The steps are: three claps, three spins, then three booty shakes. Lastly, we lay our hands and paws on the tree and are transported to the Land of Faeries and Dragons.

Will and Max's Adventure Begins

"Da Ta Da! Look! We're here!

"Ooh. I see a faerie! She is glowing!"

"Greetings Will and Max.

"I am Aine of the Light. Queen of the faeries.

"I am so happy to meet you both."

Will wonders loudly, "Hey, how do you know our names?" as he rocks side to side, giggling.

Aine smiles, "As queen, The Welcoming Tree gifts me the names of those who come through."

With eyes wide, Will exclaims, "Wow. That's terrific!"

Aine goes on, "A feast is being prepared to welcome you, but first is the dragon ride of your dreams.

"Niall will help you both ride the dragon named Blue.

"I will take you to them. The dragons live within these jeweled caves."

"This is AWESOME!" Will exclaims.

"Niall takes care of them. There he is now."

Aine introduces them, "Niall, this is Will and his dog, Max. Will and Max, this is Niall."

Niall grins, "Greetings Will and Max. Blue is ready for you."

Will jumps, "YAY! I am so excited!"
Heading further into the cave, Niall says, "Let's go meet the dragons."

Will sees two huge dragons that appear to be waiting for them and says, "Look! There they are!"

As they near the dragons, Niall introduces them, "Will and Max, this is Blue and Blaze."

Eyes sparkling, the dragons thump their tails in greeting. Max thumps his tail back, in greeting.

Will jumps up and down full of excitement, "Nice to finally meet you. I've had dreams of riding you."

Niall says, "There are three steps to dragon riding.

"Step 1 – look into the dragon's eyes so she trusts you are good. She will then lower her wings.

"Step 2 – sit on her wing and she will lift it up for you to slide into place.

"Step 3 – say, 'Soar!'

"Then you're off."

Too excited to stand still, Will says, "Got it! Let's Do This Thing! Come on Max!"

Up, up, up they go.

As Blue flips, dives, and climbs, touching the clouds, Will shouts,

"Woo-hoo! It's a Wee-eee, not a Whoa!"

Ears flapping in the wind, Max lets out an excited bark, "Rrr-uff!"

Both have a smile so big the faeries below grin.

Niall remarks, "You're brave ones Will and Max. Now, let me show you our land."

They fly all through the land, waving to faeries as they go.

Will gasps, "This place is beautiful. Wait. What's that? Look!"
He points below to an emerald, green stream. "There's a baby dragon by the water! Baby dragons can't swim!"

Blue and Blaze look down and talk to the baby. Sounding a lot like birds they say, "Sss-eee C-IIII". The baby dragon looks up and heads back to his mom, whining. His mom coos a thank you.

Niall says, "Good job Will! You helped save Lorcan. He seeks adventures beyond what is safe for his age. Water is often involved and should always be checked first, same as in your world.

"You have seen our world and helped save Lorcan. That's a great day. Let's meet the others and eat."

They land near the stream, leave the dragons to drink, and walk to a gathering of faeries.

Aine meets them. Having heard of Will saving Lorcan, she says, "Hero's greetings to you Will! We have prepared your favorite foods as well as some of ours. There is also food and drink for Max. So, as you say, 'Let's Do This Thing!'

"Like you, cheese is one of our favorites too."

Will rubs his belly saying, "Yum! My belly is grumbling."

Walking to the gathering, Will stops and sniffs. He scrunches up his nose and says, "I'm sorry. I don't mean to be rude. Smells can sometimes cause me pain."

Aine says, "Ah. That's our rabbit stew you smell. You have a strong sense of smell. I will eliminate the smells from our traditional foods."

She closes her eyes, raises her arms, and swooshes the smells away.

"Wow. That's better. Thank you." Will beams. "How nice to be considered."

While eating, they tell stories of the day and of days past. All of them agreeing that Will is forever a hero of their land. They tell him that his name, William, means, "bold protector". How fitting a name, they decide.

With the sun lowering in the sky, a young faerie cries, causing Will to covers his ears. Aine notices that Will is tired and overwhelmed. He starts to rock and repeats, "Baby don't cry. Baby don't cry. Baby don't cry."

Aine speaks kindly, "Will, we see you covering your ears, your rocking, and hear you repeating words. We notice Max is resting his head on you. We understand this means you're ready to go and we respect that."

"Please come, we will return to The Welcoming Tree so you may go home.

As you came, you will return."

Truly grateful, Will says, "Thank you for the adventure."

Aine replies, "You are most welcome William. For you are now a hero of the Land of Faeries and Dragons!"

Will and Max perform the secret code dance: three claps, three spins, then three booty shakes. They lay their hands on The Welcoming Tree and are home.

Family Characters

Aine

Niall

Lead Archer

Archer

Archer

Dragon Rider

Teacher Faerie

Wise Faerie

Archer

25

Dragon Rider

Dragon Rider

Lead Chef

Healer

Please enjoy this sneak peak of "Will's World Adventures, Book Two, Will and Max Visit the North Pole", as well as a coloring page of Max. Max is co-star of the series, just like he was in Will's life, as his service dog, for 9 years.

You can also find out more about us on Facebook, under Will's World Adventures, and on our website at www.willsworldadventures.com. There you will find more free coloring pages... you can choose to be a Dragon Rider or an Archer (maybe both?!!) by ordering our temporary tattoos! Are you into stickers? We've got those too!

Again, thank you for your support. We hope to be sharing more adventures with you!

Meredith